Pandora-X2\N4

and other short stories

Series: *Wonderful Dystopias*

Author: Michael Benassi

To my family, my partner and my cat

Dear reader,

I would like to begin by thanking you for having chosen this book among all those available in the wonderful and vast world of modern literature.

This volume was conceived as the first step towards a series of short stories which will be part of a series called *Wonderful Dystopias*. The stories in this series will be multifaceted and different, both for their length and the content, nevertheless, they will all have a fundamental characteristic: they will enable you to travel to the boundaries of space and time, to new worlds, parallel realities, near and far, often with a dystopian theme.

Short stories are usually a sort of pilot for long novels or real sagas, and mine are no exception: for each of the worlds I wanted to represent there is still so much in store, but it all depends on their reception and on which ones will create more interest.

Enjoy the reading.

Michael Benassi

Pandora-X2\N4

The world was full of bizarre jobs, but I think that the one I was about to enlist for was the most absurd and terrifying in the whole universe. I was a recent graduate who could not find work in the field of my studies and I was desperately looking for a way to achieve the economic independence I longed for. Surfing the net, through a banner, I spotted a mysterious job that intrigued me. The ad was brief, written in standard fonts and without pictures; nevertheless, I was struck by its text: "We are searching for attentive, scrupulous and fearless people for a job of fundamental importance to the security of the planet." Wow! Seriously? The SECURITY of our planet? I immediately filled out the form and, unlike the other online profiles I had filled before, I was linked to another website to take some SATs. The website was as simple as the notice, it looked like a Word file, but it included hundreds and hundreds of questions: closed-ended, open-ended, displaying of images and videos... It seemed to be a very serious and detailed inquiry. The weirdest thing, looking back, is that I can not recall any of the questions or the content of the website, however, I distinctly remember thinking that it was a huge and highly sophisticated psychological test. It lasted several

hours, I am sure about that. I started it late in the after-
noon and ended it late at night, overwhelmed and
exhausted. The next morning I was awakened by a
Skype call on the computer I had left on; I rushed to my
desk to answer: it was the Head of the Human Resources of the company who had submitted that ad. I had entered my account in the subscription form, but I had not
accepted nor entered anybody else in my Skype con-
tacts. That was funny. It was not time to think about
such things, anyway. I rubbed my face in the first wrin-
kled piece of clothing I found in my room, to wipe the
night sweat off and recover some semblance of profes-
sionalism. The interview was even stranger than the
SATs: the person I talked to was standing in dim light,
inside a dusty and crumbling room; he was wearing a
dark green uniform and a beret and he was speaking
with a distinct soviet accent. I thought that he was a man
who had great responsibilities and that I had to impress
him at any cost.

"The next morning I was awakened by a Skype call on the computer I had left on."

I remember hanging up towards the evening, so the interview must have lasted an eternity. It is a mystery why I do not remember anything from such a long conversation, but it is not the most mysterious thing I am going to tell you, that is for sure. The next morning I received an e-mail with all the instructions to get to my new workplace: they had hired me. The hardest thing was telling my parents and my friends that on that very same night I would leave for the former Soviet Union for a top-secret job I had been hired from on the internet. I think that 90% of the people wondered if I were an idiot and if I had not watched the dozens of horror films set in the middle of nowhere, beginning just like that. They even told me that I was not allowed to whine if I ended up inside a psycho's lab, since I had been warned about that. Comforting words, indeed. But at that moment I had nothing on my mind except a wish to leave. Maybe that long enlistment test and that weird interview had instilled something that manipulated my brain? I can not tell, I just know that I had never been so enthusiastic in my whole life. I left and followed all the directions to my new workplace.

I found myself in a Latvian town, in a relatively new complex of buildings. I was given a duffel bag, with a deep red uniform and a number on it, some paperwork, and other necessities. Then I was loaded on a military-derived truck from which I could not see the outside and finally fetched to the workplace. It was a four-hour journey during which the idea of the psycho's lab kept going round and round in my head. What was I thinking? Only a fool would do all of this. Luckily, before fear took over me, the truck stopped and they got me off. I was greeted by a young, blonde woman with wonderful light-blue eyes, something that clashed with the landscape behind her: a filthy and rusty metal bar led to a complex of crumbling and ruined buildings, kept under surveillance from an exceptionally tall boundary wall, adorned by razor wire, where some heavily armed soldiers were swearing and spitting on the ground. Looking at Irina's pearly-white smile, I kept wondering if that was the real world or some sort of dream. The woman did not stop asking questions about me to get to know me better.

*"A filthy and rusty metal bar led to a complex of crum-
bling and ruined buildings"*

When I found out that my room was opposite hers, I felt relieved, I loosened up a bit and I started to get closer to her. She was a woman of my age, but she had been there for a longer time, approximately five years. Apparently, that site had existed for twenty years, but, currently, she was the person who had managed to remain the most time within it and she had become a sort of mentor for the newcomers. Was five years the maximum time somebody could resist there? Perhaps I was not ready to do what I had to do. After dining together we retired to our rooms.

I was about to fall asleep in the darkness of my room when Irina knocked at my door and gave me a bracelet. She told me that it belonged to a very special person, somebody who had worked there long ago and that the small conversation we had had for the few hours we spent together, made her realize that I was the one who had to keep it. I admit, I should have questioned things, but seeing Irina in skimpy pajamas while she was giving me something, looking at me straight in the eyes, got me flustered and I could not pronounce a single word. I was stunned, I barely pronounced a "thanks a lot". She realized everything, since she smiled at me and she turned around to go back to her room; her seductive gait increased my confusion.

"When I found out that my room was opposite hers, I felt relieved."

The day after, Irina and I went to the place where I would perform my tasks. Then she delivered me into the hands of some frowning soldiers, who made me sit and watch a training video on a projector. The title read "Project Pandora-X2\Site N4". What followed was the most absurd thing I could have ever imagined in my whole life. My duty was to sit in a chair for ten hours. At the stroke of each hour, a siren would sound and, for exactly four minutes, I would have to observe what was happening in the next room, through a peephole placed on a door in front of me. When the siren stopped, I would have to get away and sit again. Whatever was happening inside that room, it was of vital importance that I never looked away, in any circumstances. What was taking place beyond that door could not hurt or harm us in any way. On the other hand, looking away could have caused terrible damage to the world population, meaning the end of the world we know. My perplexity was evident, I thought it was a joke, but the seriousness with which those soldiers were looking at me inside that dilapidated closet, made my heart go down my throat. I broke into a cold sweat.

"What... What do you see through the peephole?"

"You'll see." They answered, and they led me towards the main hall. It was old and stinky, the wooden floor was rotten, and so were the doors. The chairs were made of steel and I could see four doors, placed in a strange wall, which was not straight but made of different sides, one for each door, as if it was part of a much larger facility, which spread beyond the room we were staying in. They immediately put me to relieve a young man sitting on the right. He was pale, he seemed to have lost his hair recently, and he was skinny as a rail. He looked ill.

"All clear, I hope. You don't want to break the world, right?" Said the soldier looking at me.

I answered "All clear" and I sat down.

"After dining together we retired to our rooms."

"To go to the bathroom, to eat, drink and everything else organize yourself with the others and with the guys at the back of the room; remember, you must be here when the siren goes off. It's not a tough job, make sure you do it right." And he went away.

After a few minutes of embarrassing silence, one of the other guys asked me what my name was and we started a conversation. I relaxed a bit, but shortly after something came to my mind.

"Guys, if we talk, don't we risk forgetting to watch? Can we hear the siren?"

The guy from the other side burst out laughing.

"Don't worry, when it sounds, you'll hear it."

After a little while, a deafening sound made me jump out of the chair, and an intense red light pervaded the whole room. It sounded like an alarm of war, it was terrifying. The mere sound caused me indescribable fear and restlessness. I looked at the others, who nodded at me and gave me thumbs up to boost me. I got close to the peephole. I was frightened, but I was in a rush to watch for fear of the consequences. I leaned my face on the wet, wooden door in front of me and I watched for four minutes. I saw nothing. It was all dark and I realized I was watching another room just because I was able to glimpse a ray of dim light on the floor, which appeared to be made of wood. After the siren went off I sat down. "So, are you all right?" Asked the guy who was closer to me. The one who was laughing from the other side of the room had fallen silent and looked scared.

"The room is empty..."I answered tentatively. "The room..." but the third guy stopped me immediately: "Didn't you watch the video? You must NEVER talk about what you see in there... to anyone...it's vital."

I turned deathly pale. I had assumed that the starting point where everybody had to watch was a room. I was so wrong... in any case, I learned the lesson and the day went on in the same way for ten hours. I befriended Mark, Julius, and Henry, who would be my "colleagues" from that moment on.

"It was old and stinky, the wooden floor was rotten, and so were the doors."

The first weeks went by and I saw nothing but an empty room. My mates were watching something completely different, I supposed, because they looked disturbed, upset, or frightened by what they were viewing. It did not happen every time, just every now and then. The thing that impressed me the most was seeing Julius clinging to the door, vomiting profusely, making inhumane noises, while he was attached to the peephole. It was a really disturbing scene, luckily, I noticed it out of the corner of my eye, and I eavesdropped on his moans, since I had to stay attached to the door.

That day he remained silent for the remaining eight hours, he went to the bathroom occasionally during the breaks, presumably to vomit one more time, and he had me worried sick. What terrible things could have he been watching? And in case it occurred to me, would I be able to watch?

That night I spoke about it to Irina. We had become friends after all, and since we were next-door neighbors, we often ended up spending some time together. It was strange because in a godforsaken place like that you could not dine in a fancy restaurant or have a coffee in a chic bar to impress a girl, so I simply thought of being myself and living my crazy adventure at best, without worrying too much. She was gorgeous, playful and easy-going, therefore, besides spending time together because I genuinely liked her, I would spend my evenings with her happily, because she was able to change my surreal days with a fair amount of cheerfulness and pragmatism. We used to watch TV, play cards or play with an old console of video games she kept in her room. That day I needed to talk about what had happened. She explained to me that before her current management role, she had performed the same job and that she knew well how we felt. She told me that when the day I felt like Julius would finally come, she would stay by my side, but she implored me to remind to NEVER tell her a word about what I was seeing.

"It's horrible, I know, but it's a burden we must keep to ourselves, for good. That's why we are here." She came closer to me and she hugged me tightly. It was the first time it had happened, and her perfume inebriated me to the point that instead of being sad for the uncertain future waiting for me, I was happy like never before. How strange life is.

Another week went by and finally, I began to see something beyond the peephole. I said finally because the tension and the fear of what I could see were consuming me from the inside, even if, today, I regret my anxiety to see what was waiting for me. I started to notice weird shadows moving on the floor, where the wood could be visible in the dim light, infiltrating from who knows where. The shadows were fast and sneaky, they were moving spasmodically. It went on like this for three days. Then, the morning of the fourth day, I flinched. Suddenly a candle was lit in the back of the room. Then another and another one: apparently they lit on by themselves. The room was as I had imagined: small, rotten, and empty, with only a steel chair in the middle. The candles remained lit all day, they seemed to never consume. Then, at the last shift, the last time I had to watch before the end of my ten working hours, something that should not take place happened: I watched inside the room and I saw a person tied to the chair, bound and gagged. Judging from what he was wearing he looked like a manager: suit and tie, leather shoes, and a stylish cut. He had a showy stain of blood on the chest as if someone had punched him and the blood had dripped up to his shirt, but his face did not seem to be tumefied or swollen. What the hell was going on? I looked at the whole room to figure out where the door from which he could have come in was. There were no other doors, but, since the last time, I had not gone away. Where had he come in? Was this my actual job, perhaps? To monitor prisoners, possibly prisoners of war? Thousands of questions popped in my brain and that evening Irina noticed my sad mood and she hugged me repeatedly, stroking my head tenderly. The following morning the man was still there and he stayed there all day. During the last shift, something changed. A candle on the far right went out at once. Then the one in the middle, and, in the end, one on either side. Suddenly I saw a huge eye beyond the door looking closely at me and obscuring the view. As the eye was turning away from the peephole, the face appeared less and less human. A devilish grin of sharp little teeth seemed to be slashing a slightly hairy face, with a greenish complexion. It was a monstrous and repealing being, but very small, so much so that the kitchen knife it was holding in one hand looked like a medieval broadsword. It moved like an ape towards the

hapless manager in the middle of the room, never looking away from me, and it cut the man's throat from side
to side, smiling. I had a retch of vomit and I shrieked, but
the racket of the sirens drew out my screaming, and I
doubt that somebody heard it.

Finally, I understood what those loud and annoying sirens served as. Initially, their noise sounded fearsome
and unnatural, but it probably helped to protect and iso-
late ourselves from the others during the shift. The
thing that struck me the most was that in the last days,
whatever was inside the room, appeared to know when
it was the end of my shift, and it left me more doubtful
and terrified every time. I did not dine that evening, and,
again, I got Irina's attentions, which, I must admit, chee-
red me up. I was not remotely prepared for what was
going to happen shortly thereafter.

Nothing appeared inside the little room for a couple of
days, then, all of a sudden, a blonde woman in an elegant
dress showed up. She was motionless in the middle of
the room and she seemed dazed. Shortly after she suffered the same treatment as the man of some days before.
But I had already seen that woman somewhere, so I
searched on the internet and I found out that she was a

quite well-known actress in the world of TV series. The problem was that the woman had just died: that very day she had been found in her hotel room with symptoms of an overdose and the race to the hospital had not saved her life. At that point, I lost it. If that girl was physically present and even dead in another place in the world, with symptoms of an overdose and not of violent death, and her corpse had been found intact, who the hell was that person I was watching every day in that little room? A doppelganger? A clone specially created by the soldiers? Was she the actual actress and her death had just been a government setup? Unreal holographic images inside that little room were projected for a strange experiment, or were we lab rats? Was it all in my head and was I going crazy? I thought the woman was a look-alike, and that all the rest was just my paranoia, mostly to remain calm, and not because I believed it; however, when some pictures of the actress on a stretcher, taken off the hotel she was staying in popped up, I shivered when I noticed that she was wearing the same identical elegant red dress I had seen in the little room. She starred in a post-apocalyptic TV series, consequently, that dress was not a well-known costume, but her own one. Gruesome.

The day after, something even more awful occurred: during the first siren of the day a young guy showed up in the little room, facing away from me, looking familiar. When he turned, my blood ran cold: he was a dear friend of mine, a former college roommate, we had lived many adventures together and we were friends for life. He too was standing, but, unlike the young actress, the look in his eye appeared sad and thoughtful and he seemed to have red spots on both his wrists. Panic took over, I knew what was going to happen to my friend in the little room, but there was nothing I could do. As the siren stopped, I twirled around and I ran to the soldiers, telling them that I had to make a phone call immediately, screaming and pawing. The biggest one grabbed me by the neck, looked at me in the eye, and said, in a strangely peaceful way, that had nothing to do with the rough ways he was using to block me physically:

"I know you've seen something that upset you, boy, and I know you'd like to call someone to tell them something. It has already happened before. Good Lord, you don't know how many things happened in here. But you can't, boy. You know that there is a strict code of conduct to observe here. You know that you're doing something that has to do with the whole of mankind. Calm down, sit, and come back to your job. Whatever you want to do, it won't change anything."

His strong grip made me dizzy, and I realized that I had no chance of going away.

I went back to my place and, during the following shift of the siren, I saw my friend meeting his destiny.

Once I got back to my room I immediately opened the mail and, already hopeless, I opened a message from my former college roommates, who were informing me that my dear friend had been found lifeless in his bathroom, with his wrists severed. He had probably come down with severe depression, caused by his recent personal problems. I felt like shit. But not like an ordinary shit, the biggest shit in the world. Not only would I have been able to do something from this absurd and godforsaken place I found myself in if they had let me make a phone call at the right moment, but I could at least have gotten in touch more often once we finished university. Maybe

I would have realized that he needed help. Maybe. That sucks.

"Every day I saw groups of people coming from all over
the world, of different ethnicities and religions, who indulged in barbarous acts against other human beings."

That evening I was totally upset and I did not talk. I wanted to tell Irina everything, but I knew that I could not and that doing it meant getting her into trouble, so I shut up and I hugged her. I was so in need of comfort and I burst into tears. She waited for me to stop sighing, then she pulled me away and she looked at me in the eye; then she came close again and she kissed me. My heart started to throb, and in a moment, I was no more thinking about the horrible things I was experiencing. I took her forcefully, made her lie down, and started to undress her. Her smooth and fair skin shone on her fiery red sexy lingerie, and it scented indescribably, while I was totally lost and intoxicated by her. When the crucial moment came I realized that I did not have condoms with me and, honestly, the last thing I wanted to make in that godforsaken place was a mess.

She immediately grasped what was unsettling me, she looked at me, softly and sensually, and said:

"Don't worry, getting pregnant in this place is not possible. I know it's hard to believe, but it's true. Do you trust me?" And she smiled at me.

Faced with such a beautiful and sweet girl, completely naked, who was waiting for me only, what could I do? I believed, also because I genuinely trusted her. I felt we had a special connection since the day we had met. Needless to say, it was wonderful, and it relieved me from all the terrible thoughts that had been pervading my mind until that night. From that moment on, no matter what happened, I knew I only had to survive psychologically till evening, because then I would see Irina and all the rest would be wiped away.

She would be my lifeline and my purpose, my light in the darkness.

And, unfortunately, I was really in need of light in the darkness. In the following days and weeks, I saw more and more less logical things, which were devouring my mind.

Everything showed up inside that little room: I saw some of my long-dead relatives being brutally murdered by hooded men, and then I witnessed unprecedented violence committed on apparently random people. Every day I saw groups of people coming from all over the world, of different ethnicities and religions, who indulged in barbarous acts against other human beings: young, old, children, and even animals. I witnessed homicides, tortures, and rapes, committed on more or less innocent people by other people of all kinds and social backgrounds. It was terrible, and I risked fainting more than once.

I used to vomit every day and I stopped eating, I was wasting away, and so were my colleagues. I wondered why they did not analyze our biometric parameters or our daily psychological conditions, seeing us in such a state. Perhaps nobody cared, perhaps that was the actual scope, or maybe they were doing it in some way, unbeknownst to us.

Irina knew what was happening to me, but we could not talk about it, therefore we tried to feel well during the time we spent together. She made me listen to some audio files she had recorded on a cd: they came from a not well-known *Youtuber*, who was trying to bring positivity in everybody's life through motivational speeches. Surprisingly, those speeches helped me a lot, and I realized that, despite everything, I was lucky. I had to witness horrible things and I had to resist losing my humanity while seeing them, nevertheless, I had a wonderful woman by my side and a simple but full life. This gave me the kick to go on, if not with a smile on my face, at least without the risk of going insane. Listening to those speeches together and talking about them, helped both of us, and we became even closer.

Then something even more unbelievable and bizarre happened: I stopped seeing anything through the peephole. It did not seem to be the same room with the lights off, it really was the dark cosmic void. Black, pitched dark. Frankly, I felt relieved. A lot. It went on like this for several days, until I suddenly started to glimpse something even more absurd: I could see a purple whirlwind. It was very small at first sight, but then it grew bigger and bigger until it took all the visual space the lens I was watching through allowed me to have. It was intense purple, permeated by tiny sparkling lights, creating the impression that they were moving in spirals. It looked like a *wormhole*, a door to another universe, or something like that. It gave me a strange and alarming feeling of powerlessness and enormity, however, I tremendously preferred that whirlwind to the scenes of violence I had seen before. After all, nothing that I saw made sense, so I might as well keep observing what appeared to be a good wormhole, harmless, albeit disarming, rather than criminals and vicious killers or crazy critters.

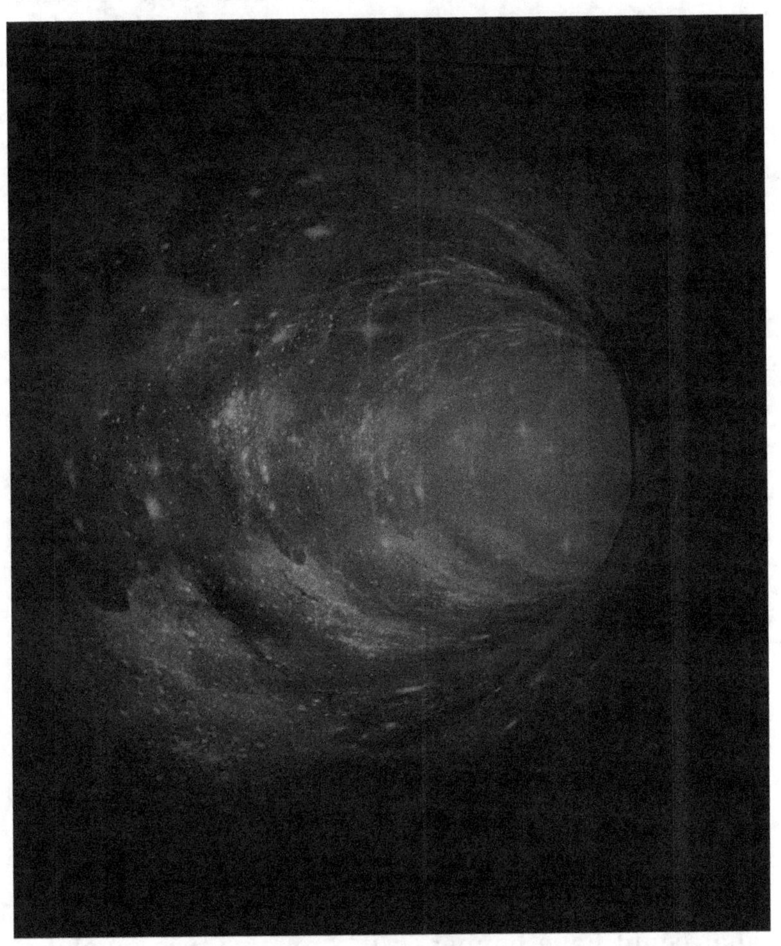

"It looked like a wormhole, a door to another universe, or something like that."

For several weeks I saw the same thing again and again, and I started to relax a bit until something that upset me seriously happened one more time. It was our final shift when I distinctly heard screams and shots amid the uproar caused by the siren. I noticed a turmoil out of the corner of my eye, then the siren went out and we stepped away from our stations. The soldiers were forcibly blocking Mark, who was trying to smash the door. Actually, I had had the same instinct more than once because of the atrocious things I had been witnessing, however, I suspect that my brain was in defense mode, due to which, everything I was seeing was not considered real, but just as a movie. Because of that, I had always managed to control the urge to step in. But I can imagine what could have happened. Mark must have seen some of the atrocious actions inflicted on somebody he knew. Perhaps a relative. Some of those scenes were themselves unsustainable, I can only imagine what could have happened if a relative was involved, maybe if he or she was still alive. While he was being dragged away, he managed to scream:

"My little sister! My sister! How can you-" they gagged him straightaway.

I do not dare to imagine what he could have seen, but unfortunately, I knew what took place there too well. But I still did not know whether it was real or not, and, if yes, in which way. That evening I saw Mark leaving, and I managed to barely say goodbye to him through the window of the vehicle where they had loaded him. The following day he had already been replaced by a new guy. But something had changed since the previous evening. I did not see the whirlwind anymore; I started to see wonderful landscapes in its place. It seemed like I was looking through the peephole of a holiday home, overlooking a beach, other times a lake, or a snow-covered landscape... I must admit, it was gorgeous, and I could not wait for the siren to go off to watch it again. I got sucked in as if it were a TV series, a cigarette, a drug. I wanted more and more of it.

"I started to see wonderful landscapes in its place."

The new guy was not fitting in well, he seemed to suffer a lot for his job. Something similar to what Mark had experienced took place, but without the same fuss. I did not understand the events very well, because everything occurred during the unceasing sound of the siren, nevertheless, he too was taken away. The day after, I found myself observing a charming mountain scenery, in the middle of nature, between two lush, emerald-green valleys. A rivulet flew from the right and it approximately reached my feet beyond the door, while a peaceful and bucolic atmosphere permeated the whole scene. I could have smelled it, and that was weird because it seemed almost feasible. Suddenly, I saw a giant train popping out of the valley, it was coming at a breakneck speed right in my direction, puffing black and white smoke and increasing evermore its run. My brain made a tremendous effort to let me stay still in my viewpoint, instead of scaring me off. When it finally arrived where I was standing, the siren went off. I, as I used to do, I waited for a matter of seconds and I broke away from the door. As soon as I did it, the door shook lightly, as if it had been hit by something from the other side. It was such an imperceptible movement that I thought I had imagined everything due to suggestion. However, at the end of the shift, I saw the soldiers coming closer to my door, along with some scientists wearing a white lab coat, who were holding several weird tools. I hardly swallowed and I went back to my room.

In the following days, the zone beyond the peephole darkened again until an increasingly shining white light started to brighten the whole zone, gradually and more intensely from time to time. In the end, you could see an endless stretch of white, with only a single demarcation line that seemed to define the sky and the ground, but both were white. I started to discern some slender figures walking towards me, and every time I looked at them, they appeared to be closer. When they were very, very close, they placed themselves in a semicircle in front of the door. They looked like creatures coming from another planet and judging from their features and clothes, you could guess they were female specimens. The long and slender fingers popped out their robes, as white as their skin, while the big hood pariallly masked their facial features. They started to make gestures and movements which reminded me of *Tai-Chi*, and it seemed that each of them had a precise sequence to re-peat. They went on like this for a few days, and I noticed that some of their movements corresponded to tremors of the door or to strange noises in the room I was staying in. It seemed that they were trying to affect what stayed on our side of the door. I knew that I could not say anything about what I was seeing, but I warned the soldiers about the fact that I had the impression that there were strange movements and vibrations at the door. They took me seriously since, apparently, I was considered a veteran observer. Nevertheless, they did not detect anything abnormal.

Then, during an observation shift, all the creatures in a circle made a gesture in unison, but just at that time, the siren went out. I used to wait a few seconds before going away after the power off, just to be sure, but in that case, I had a strange feeling. It had not been four minutes since the siren had started sounding. It had been two and a half, three, maybe. Why had it already gone out? Suddenly an enormous eye appeared in front of the lens and then I understood. I started yelling at everyone not to break away from the peephole, that time had not run out yet, while I could hear the soldiers behind me bustling and getting ready for something. With the corner of my eye, I saw that two of my mates who had broken away from their door were on the point of getting closer again, but a huge dark blade with green and neon blue veins pierced the door and stabbed them.

Since I had kept watching through the peephole, I saw a creature hitting the door with all their strength, and it started to move in a very alarming way. I knew I had to remain there, I did not know why, but I knew I had to stay there.

Suddenly, I saw a beam coming from one of those hooded creatures.

At the same time, I heard a bump and felt a sharp pain in the back of my neck, and I collapsed.

When I woke up, the four doors were open and an immense light came from each of them. The floor was covered in empty shell casings, blood, and corpses. I heard Irina crying and screaming my name desperately, I turned and I saw her running in my direction, slick with blood. She pulled me up and reassured me, saying that the blood was not hers and that we had to go away immediately. They loaded us on a white helicopter that I had never seen at the base, although I had wondered what a heliport was for, and we left that place straight away.

This is only an extract of what happened to me: from the very first moment I had arrived, I had been writing a diary with the details of everything I was seeing, day by day, and I will keep writing it in the next place they are going to bring me. I will leave this manuscript hidden, hoping that someone will find and publish it. If I can, I will make sure that, besides this brief document, the whole diary will be found: I still do not know what we are doing, but the people of this world deserve to know what is happening in these places. Whatever it is.

"They loaded us on a white helicopter that I had never seen at the base."

JusticeIntegrated

*"Citizens had rebelled vehemently, as we learned from the
history books and the famous accounts of the triennium
2027-2030.""*

I had to understand, I had to realize how everything had begun, give a logical and rational explanation to everything happening to me. To the feelings I had and to my mind, which seemed completely changed, in such a short time and apparently without a break.

Let's start from the beginning.

It was the day of my twenty-fifth birthday and, like almost all the twenty-five-year-old guys who want to be considered cool, I had gone to the local integrated bureaucracy office to enable the justice reform App (JutsiceIntegrated) on my smart assistant. Since 2030, in fact, every young man in his prime could not wait to access that app, and anxiously waited for the day of his birthday to queue at the local office, just to have their access to the system authorized.

The app had arrived with the justice reform of a few years before, and it was basically used to entrust the law to the citizens. The citizens of 2030, in fact, tired and furious because of the wave of crimes, rapes, murders, and thefts inflicted on the ordinary people who struggled to make ends meet to feed their families, had rebelled vehemently, as we learned from the history books and the famous accounts of the triennium 2027-2030.

The subsequent fall of the government and the signing of the new hardline had been inevitable.

Since that day, everything has changed. Before the reform, the state of things in the streets was unsustainable: I was a child and I do not remember much, but I recall the criminality and the decadence the cities were oozing with very well, even if they had become part of the daily life that many pretended, or maybe believed, was normal. Like a toad, when it is put in a pot at room temperature: it does not realize that the stove has been turned on until the water boils, when it is too late. After the riots, the justice reform had ensured that the crimes were waning, but the statistics showed something wrong. Actually, they showed a strange pattern, however, after the huge expenditure, the efforts, and the propaganda, nobody would ever admit that something did not add up.

"The subsequent fall of the government and the signing of the new hardline had been inevitable."

So, that day, I finally had access to the platform. Like everybody else, I was authorized to access the database of the crimes currently under trial. For all those criminals, the first level of judgment, the magistrature, had already decreed their guilt. It was up to us citizens to decide the sentence. It was a revolutionary idea: all criminals were convicted or found innocent by legal experts, speedy trials were set up, with a much-toughened law compared to the past, in which their guilt beyond a reasonable doubt was defined, as well as a series of possible penalties to be imposed, from the mildest to the most dreadful ones, which would be voted by the citizens. Obviously, in order to have access to the app, the citizens had to have specific characteristics, automatically verified during the several school aptitude and psychological tests over the years, but that meant that almost everyone could access it.

The app featured a social media-like interface, where you could easily scroll from one crime to the other and quickly select your own choice. In theory, to choose, you had to consult all the files provided: from text files to audio and video files, even if there was no shortage of tricks and bugs to "make it fast" and sentence straigh-

taway.

*"The JutsiceIntegrated app featured a social media-like
interface"*

And there I was, ready for my first sentence. I wanted to sentence that crime since I had heard about it on the local news. It was horrible: a gang rape perpetrated against a woman who was coming home from work. The ferocity and the cruelty of that crime had upset me, and, honestly, after all the news I had heard, I just wanted to see them DYING. And... yes, I wanted to be one of the people who had pushed the "death penalty" button. I still remember that day as it was yesterday, I will never forget it. I did not have a clue about what I was about to experience. The rapists had recorded everything that had been done, it was all documented. In order to sentence, you needed to watch everything. I thought that it was better that way, so I would be even more certain about my choice. I was so wrong... I watched the full video. The poor woman was first insulted in the streets, then threatened, and finally dragged to a secluded spot. There, five people abused her in the most horrible way you can imagine. When you hear about rapes, the very thought horrors you, but seeing such a thing with your own eyes changes your life. It fucks your brain. Thinking that a human being can commit something so heinous makes you want to disappear from the face of the earth.

First, the rape lasted forever. It did not last five minutes, it went on for so long. There were endless and devastating moments, in which the woman screamed, writhed, and begged her torturers and her God for mercy. She vomited, slick with blood and tears, going from motionless silence to screams of pain and mercy and then to silence again. I did not believe that anything like that could exist, but I was witnessing it with my very own eyes. The look of fun in their eyes, the laughter, the bangs and the abuses they were committing on that woman made me dizzy. I did not know what was going on, I felt bad. I vomited and I fell on my back with the headphones still on my ears, in the silence of my room. When I recovered my senses, I clicked on the attackers' profile and I chose "death penalty" for all five, it did not matter who the brain was, who had recorded and who had done what. Five deaths, I opted for the most painful way, the injection of the "ASKPEX" compound. It was going to be a twenty-four hours agony, broadcast live on the app for those who wanted to witness it. I could not wait to see it and laugh all the time. They say that the injection of such a compound is the most painful thing a human

being can experience and that it has been made specifi-
cally to prevent fainting, which is something the body
usually does when the pain becomes unbearable. They
say the sensation can be compared to being turned inside out like a glove, while endless, incandescent pins
perforate you spasmodically, submerged in a lava ocean
with a fire burning your body from the inside. At that
moment, it did not seem enough, but it was the maximum you could choose.

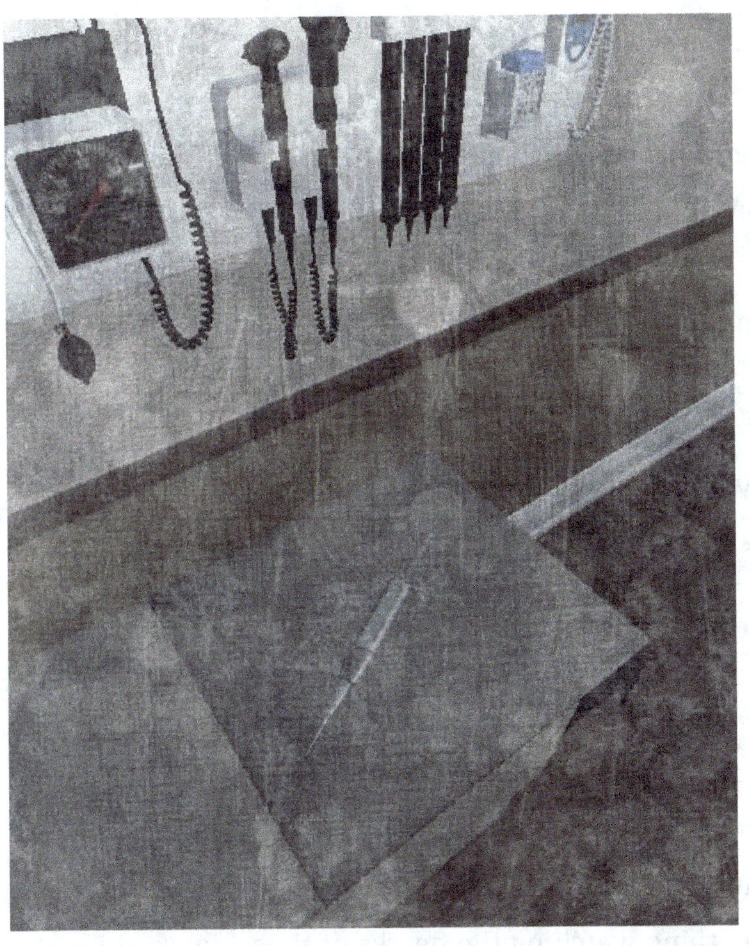

"I opted for the most painful way, the injection of the "ASKPEX" compound. It was going to be a twenty-four hours agony, broadcast live on the app for those who wanted to witness it."

That was my first experience with the app. I must admit that after seeing the attackers' agony for a few minutes, I stopped using it, and I wondered if I would be able to watch another contribution to sentence somebody else. The video of the woman's agony had been truly horrible and I kept thinking about it, it was like I had seen it in front of me. I carried part of the woman's pain inside of me, I wanted to know how she was doing, help her and apologize to her on behalf of the human race because no living being should ever suffer what she had suffered. What they have been saying on the internet for decades is indeed true: "you cannot unsee what you have seen". In other words, once you have seen something, you saw it, and whatever damage it can do to your psyche, it is too late to come back. Perhaps, among the tests for the app usage, they should verify if the person is too empathic or if the vision of certain contents could have repercussions. I do not know. The fact is that I did not feel anything watching the deaths of those damned beasts, and that scared me further. Moreover, I did not feel responsible for that decision. Their actions had led them to die in that way, not us who had voted.

A couple of years later something upsetting happened again. I had a childhood friend I used to play football within the neighborhood with: he was arrested and brought to trial. His trial was very, very complex and since he was someone I used to know, even if I had not seen him for a long time, I decided to watch everything, otherwise, I would regret it in the future. After all, I could always choose to sentence him to the minor penalty.

In the time elapsed between my first experience with the app and this last one, I rarely logged in and I used the judgment only for nonviolent crimes, mainly related to the world of finance, illegal trafficking, and other crimes, and I must admit that I learned a lot from the files I read in such cases and I usually spent time to choose the most considered penalty according to me, without any particular repercussions. This one was different, however, a lot different, unfortunately. I had been following my former playmate on social media, even if, as I mentioned before, I had not seen him for a long time, and I had noticed that he was particularly active on the JusticeIntegrated app. He had continuously been sharing stats about it, completed objectives (there was a reward system for those who sentenced numerous daily penalties), and took pride in his severe but wise choices. He had changed the way he dressed, he got awfully thin, you could see a clear shift in the photographs and, by retracing his profile, that shift appeared to be both physical and psychological. What the hell had he done to be brought to trial? I did not have a clue, so I logged in and, again, I found myself facing something I wish I did not know, against my will.

This time there were no videos, thank goodness. There were many, too many photos, instead.

Apparently, the boy in question (yes, I am distancing myself from him) was wandering at night along a country road, on foot, alone and with a shoulder bag. A local family - father, mother, and three children - on their way back from an out-of-town dinner, stopped to help him, because he appeared to be in a confusional state.

It was later revealed that he never slept at home and that the wandering occurred every night. The family was found slaughtered on the side of the road the following day. The bag was full of proper and improper weapons, instruments of torture, and other amenities.

He had slaughtered them like pigs, and only he knew which other insanities he had inflicted on those unfortunate people, dead or maybe alive, since not even the Forensic Science Department figured it out, given the state in which they were. Nobody said it aloud, but I searched all his posts, and his recent deeds looked like the sum of all the filth he had seen during the years he had been using JusticeIntegrated. And what did he say in court? Only one thing: "I'm begging you, give me ASKPEX" I gave it to him.

At that time I started to ask myself more questions: when I learned about certain things human beings were able to do, I felt sick, very sick. "We" were doing that. But was it right to lock me in a sort of bubble, or did I have to change myself instead, and be conscious and informed of what people do? And again, had my former playmate always been like that, or his overexposure to violence had completely destroyed him, inside and outside, changing him to the point he had become himself a monster? And what if that was slowly happening to everybody using the app? Was it possible that no psychologist was working on that aspect? Or maybe somebody was working on it, and it was all a great social experiment? What the hell was going on?

I started to do some research, I had to know. The idea of letting the people decide on a fair penalty was wonderful, unique, and revolutionary. It really put the power in the right place. But what if it had been poorly and hastily executed and nobody wanted to admit that? Or what if it was a great but utopian idea, because of the very nature of men, and therefore unfeasible in real life? It existed, and stopping it seemed impossible.

I started to investigate some cases which were highly disputed, and I realized that sometimes the evidence was obviously "strange". Some questionable parts were missing, video and audio files seemed ambiguous or they presented subtle and imperceptible signs of retouching. The worst part was that some of those signs of inconsistencies were deeply hidden in the evidence I had myself assessed for some of the past judgments, and I had not noticed anything in the first place. I approached a community of people whose aim was to debunk the issues of JusticeIntegrated to terminate its use or at least revise it from the start to regulate it properly. But to do so, using the app was obligatory since if you want to tell what are the issues you must use it on an regular basis.

It has been eight years since that moment and I am exhausted. JusticeIntegrated is still there, powerful as ever, and with even more advanced functions than before. The death penalty through ASKPEX is the most common one by now, even for crimes that were previously judged to be minor. Small groups of friends binge-watch criminals dying on live streams.

"The death penalty through ASKPEX is the most common one by now, even for crimes that were previously judged to be minor."

The app has become more social and integrated into the daily life of everyone. Almost all the people with whom I shared my thorough examination of the inconsistencies of the app have been arrested, locked up in a mental institution, disappeared or changed their lives. There are only a few of us and I am no longer sure of anything. I lost twenty kilos, I sleep every other day, four hours at the most. I am pale and paranoid, sometimes I am not alert and I am not able to think straight. I am in jail and I am waiting for the verdict. I saw the videos, I saw myself with my hands covered in blood, while I was stabbing that policeman. But it was not me, I do not think so. I mean, the image was blurred, I do not remember it. I mean, if it had been me... I would remember it... because...because. I do not know if... help... I am innocent, anyway.

Yes. It is false and fabricated evidence. I suppose. I do not think anyone will care, anyway.

The verdict has come. ASKPEX. Maybe it is only fair that I try it on myself, after all the people I indirectly gave it to by pushing the button. Farewell.

Alien Invasion

"I'm begging you, let us live, you've already taken every-thing from us....why are you doing this? You've de-stroyed and robbed us... go away and at least spare our lives."

His words echoed like a prayer in a holy place, but nothing mattered to the invader. He lift the visor of his space helmet and, with a look of defiance mixed with contempt, answered him:

"I'll let you live because you are nothing, just like the rest of you, after all. Beat it!"

Januth took up his robes, still dirty with the pain of his slaughtered friends, and fled to the mountains, crying and rueing the day the alien invader had landed.

They came from nowhere, on an ordinary day of an or-dinary year.

Life used to be quiet in his village before, everyone did what they could to get by, but everyone was happy. The connections with the main metropolis were common and comfortable, and the news traveled fast thanks to the technological development of the most recent years. Januth belonged to a group of modest friends, engaged in the agricultural arts, with no big dreams except for having a quiet life with a happy family. Thus, the day the news of the arrival of an alien invader arrived in the country, everyone stuck to the screens to know more about it, and soon the mockery towards those who were afraid to speak about it turned into sheer terror in everybody's eyes.

They came on enormous spaceships, each carrying different symbols on the bridge, but all of them were white and gigantic, apparently made of unknown and extra-resistant materials. The traditional weapons could not compete against those monstrosities and, above all, once they were detected, they were so close that they were impossible to stop. The most absurd thing was that, before all this, aliens were often mentioned among Januth's friends, both in the city and in the country. They wondered if they would come in peace or if they would try to make some kind of deal or kidnap the most important politicians in secret. Nobody expected that they would actually arrive, all guns blazing, destroying everything they found without a reason. They did not even try to send an ambassador, a coded message, or talk to a politician. They did nothing but slaughter, since day one. They had thought that a blitz attack was the quickest and safest way to spread fear and win without the possibility of response.

It was truly hell.

Dwellers from the largest cities were the less fortunate since they immediately became the target of the most devastating attacks. Or maybe they were the luckiest ones since they did not have to experience all that came after.

The spaceships flew above the city centers and the squares in profound silence and dropped giant bombs that turned into incandescent balls of energy and debris, which devastated the buildings and tore through every living being in the area. Once razed to the ground, cities were then plundered by those called the "raiders": they were soldiers chosen among the strongest and most valiant of their race, with their heavy and hardwearing jumpsuits, against which the weak and improvised weapons of the unsuspecting citizens who had just survived huge explosions were powerless. To make matters worse, each of them was followed by ravenous beasts, trained to attack on command every hapless living being designated to be a pray by their owners. Our people were literally devoured by those beasts, and those who managed to escape from them were simply disintegrated by the brute force of the raiders and their weapons. They were huge.

Every alien's size was at least twice any average citizen's size. What is more, those had been recruited for their force and brutality. It was not a war, it was a massacre.

"The spaceships flew above the city centers and the squares in profound silence and dropped giant bombs that turned into incandescent balls of energy and debris, which devastated the buildings and tore through every living be-ing in the area."

Any politicians' attempt to communicate with the enemy proved to be vain. And not for a lack of communication. No. They spoke our same language. No one could tell if they had studied it or if they were wearing a simultaneous translation device. Nonetheless, their ravenous mouths spoke words understandable even to us. And that was dreadful. They had CHOSEN to behave that way. They had DECIDED to wipe out an entire race, a planet.

After he had arrived in his village in the mountains, Januth took shelter in the usual underground bunker converted from the village's youth meeting place, as soon as the war broke out.

As he arrived inside, he hugged his girlfriend Jackih with bitter tears and he said that he loved her with all his heart. The time had finally come. His village had to make an effort to fight one last time, or surrender to the enemy. For all they knew, surrendering meant dying. From the very little information spread after the outbreak of the war, the aliens were taking no prisoners. They were not interested in prisoners, they were only a burden. Apparently, they were there to exterminate.

"What do they want from us, Januth? Why are they doing all this? Whatever they want they already know they can get it, why do they keep killing us?"

"Maybe they just want what lies under our feet" replied the young man, still upset from what he had just experienced.

After a moment of reflection, where the young people who had recently died on the side of Januth were commemorated, the preparations for the counter-offensive began.

The smartest boy in the village, someone who used to read a lot and have an alert mind, had the idea. They would have to exploit the conformation of the few access routes to the village to set a trap in which very heavy rocks would fall straight on the raiders' heads and blocked the access for good.

That could be long-term suicide, but they could buy some time. Hope would do the rest.

The schemes and the maps were ready, everyone was smiling and hopeful. It was unbelievable to think that, in hard times, even being faced with the possibility of dying became a chance of smiling, thanks to hope. All the sad moments of daily life, born out of worthless nonsense, meant something new then. Whoever lived in that dark bunker would gladly turn back to a few months before, even on the most miserable day they had ever lived, because you never realize how lucky you are until you face the true horror. But they were all there, smiling and hopeful, ready to do what was necessary for the sake of each other.

Jakih's duty was to remain with the youngest and protect them with her life until the end. She greeted Januth one more time, as she had already done earlier, remarking how much she loved him.

"Thanks for all you gave me in this life. We were supposed to get married soon and have children. If I had known what we were going to have to go through, I'd have spent less time fighting with you and more time enjoying the happiness we used to have. But in the end, the best parts of our life together were the little quarrels and the daily challenges. I'd give everything, everything to go back to those times. You are my whole life and no matter what happens, wherever you are, wherever we end up being next, I will always love you. Thank you."

Januth burst into tears, he kissed her passionately and told her one thing only:

"You saved my life when you chose to love me, many years ago. Now I'll do everything to save the lives of all the people here and, if I fail, we'll meet in the afterlife. I'll find you. Thank you."

Everybody turned towards the door when they heard a blood-curling noise that froze everyone.

TOC-TOC

Silence

TOC-TOC

Again

The semi-metallic voice of one of those damned aliens echoed behind the door.

"Open the door!"

Januth promptly pushed Jackih and all the children in the farthest corner of the room. He moved all the strongest young people in the middle of the room and the adults on both sides, a desperate formation to try to save the situation.

"I'm alone, I'm here to help you, I'm begging you, open the door!"

Nobody trusted him, but on the other hand, there was not much hope left.

"If you don't believe me kill me, you'll have no resistance from me. I can't do what I'm doing anymore."

They let Januth decide.

Although young, he was considered the cleverest of the group, and everyone trusted him. Maybe for his affable but persuasive attitude, maybe because he had proved his worth more than once. He was not strong, but he was intelligent and quick, and that had helped him many times in his life. Now more than ever.

Januth decided to proceed, but he nodded at Jackih first: she was staring at him from the back of the room. They agreed with each other.

When the group slowly opened the door, they glimpsed only one alien. He was huge. Without any doubt one of the biggest ever seen. He was not carrying his fiery best with him, indicating that he had decided to help them.

He immediately took his space helmet off, and, when finally everyone was able to look at him closely, they noticed that the aliens owned an electronic device that translated their native language simultaneously.

"We don't have much time, all the raiders left in the area are coming, because they know this is the last village to be taken over. They think you are more in number and they're bringing all the weapons here. If you manage to defeat them and take their supplies, your counter-attack could start from this village. They have enough weapons to fight off troops for a good while and to build similar weapons if you can."

"..."

Januth was immobile and did not know what to say, partly for the fear inherent in the situation, also increased by the acrid smell the alien exuded that frightened everybody. They had already smelt that stench, when the aliens had attacked them hand to hand, and it was a death omen.

Finally, after he came to his senses, Januth muttered something, and asked coldly:

"Why should we trust you? Why do you want to help us and betray your people? We could never forgive someone who betrays us to help you."

"Neither could we. I want to help you and die in doing so. Only then will I forgive myself for the horrible things I did."

"But why did you do them? Why are you here?"

"You must know that all the resources on my planet have been depleted. We have stripped our world of all it had and we turned it into an awful, overcrowded, and arid place. Living there is hell. Your planet is wonderful and our monarchs have decided to invade and colonize it. We raiders have been deceived. We were exhausted by hunger and poverty and we were promised a safe place for our families; they told us you were violent and inferior beings, that our coexistence was not possible because you had slaughtered our peacekeepers. But none of that was true and I found out too late. We were brainwashed by the substances they had given us and they sent us to massacre you. I beg your forgiveness. When I realized that, despite the obvious physical diffe-rences, we were alike in every way, it was too late. Look beyond our appearance that you find monstrous and you'll see that we're similar. I too have a person I love and children, and it pains me to die here and not be able to greet them one last time. But I realized that they will never have their own place. They fooled me, there is no space for everybody. Only the monarchs and their henchmen will come to colonize. Our families will stay and die on that damned planet."

Everyone in the room was dismayed. They all realized what their grandparents had always narrated but that no one had ever understood: the horror of war. There is a massive story behind each fighter, a multitude of events behind every person, and only despair behind the violence.

The alien had brought four explosive devices with him, those used to destroy the cities; they could have perfectly worked with Januth and the others' plan. In a few hours they set up everything and the alien gave his new allies all the instructions on everything they had to know in case he did not survive. He asked them to remember and pass down his name and his family's name to the future generations in case he did not make it so that his act of love could have been the symbol of a new renaissance and of the fact that not all aliens are ravenous beasts who came to massacre.

The moment had come. Too soon, the last device had not been properly positioned yet, but that was the way it was supposed to be. They gathered all the fighters as bait in the center of the village, but, as soon as the enemy's synchronized attack

broke out, they exploded the devices taking shelter in the bunker. All hell broke loose and for a few moments, everything was silent. Then some screams could be heard more clearly and everybody went out to see what was going on. It was an apocalyptic scene, everything got destroyed, the enemy's troops had been exterminated, except for a large group which, no one knows how, had managed to escape the destruction. They were a lot. The alien drew a huge sharp weapon, it was used during close combat, and seldom did someone draw it. Once the others recovered from the initial astonishment, they drew their weapons as well and began to attack him. It was a terrible scene.

The acrid smell of the fighting aliens was tremendous and their giant and hairy bodies smacked at every blow, with splashes of bodily fluids which permeated all the surrounding area. The alien's strength came from his love for his family and a greater purpose, and so he managed to subdue all his former comrades, also thanks to a beast that had begun to fight at his side against the other beasts that were attacking him. Januth and his people were already celebrating, when the alien turned towards them and they noticed that his white spacesuit had been pierced repeatedly and his own bodily fluid was dripping everywhere. Even the beast that had fought at his side was in a bad state, but it had won. The alien came close to Januth and Jackih left the shelter to see what was happening. As the alien collapsed in his new friend's arms, he pulled out a strange pictogram from the spacesuit and gave it to Januth, who was holding him with difficulty, due to his enormous size.

"Here, I've served my purpose. Now remember me and be proud of who you are. Show everyone what I gave to you and spread the word: not all the invaders are ravenous beasts, tell your children and grandchildren about what my beloved family and I did for love. And I implore you, I implore you, forgive me."

After having said that, he closed his eyes and breathed his last breath, hugging his beast, who also departed this life.

A candid tear rolled down Jackih's green cheekbone as she looked at Januth's purple eyes. He stood up and, looking at the lifeless bodies of the alien and his beast he said:

"We'll remember Diego and his family forever. Marta, Luigi, and Caterina will be proud of him, whether they know or not what happened here. We learned to fear and hate the terrestrials, but down there, where they come from, there are beings like us, who love and live. We must rise again and send them away, but always remember not to make their same mistake, not to let despair turn us into what they have become. We will bury Diego with his dog Max so that they can rest in peace forever."

"We'll remember Diego and his family forever. We will bury Diego with Max so that they can rest in peace forever."

-Memorial site.

www.ingramcontent.com/pod-product-compliance
Lightning Source LLC
Chambersburg PA
CBHW072119150726

47999CB00005B/2028